This book belongs to

This educational book was created in cooperation with Children's Television Workshop, producers of SESAME STREET. Children do not have to watch the television show to benefit from this book. Workshop revenues from this book will be used to help support CTW educational projects.

Featuring Jim Henson's Sesame Street Muppets

Children's Television Workshop/Funk & Wagnalls

Authors

Linda Hayward
Deborah Kovacs
Jeffrey Moss
Michaela Muntean
Pat Tornborg

Illustrators

Richard Brown
Tom Cooke
Robert Dennis
Joe Ewers
Tom Leigh
Maggie Swanson

 Published in the United States of America by Western Publishing Company, Inc., Racine, WI 53404, in conjunction with Children's Television Workshop. Distributed by Funk & Wagnalls, Ramsey, NJ. Manufactured in the United States of America.

0-8343-0081-8 1 2 3 4 5 6 7 8 9 0

A Parents' Guide to PEOPLE IN MY NEIGHBORHOOD

What do your children want to be when they grow up? One day it's a fire fighter, the next it's a doctor. The popular Sesame Street song "People in Your Neighborhood" introduces children to various occupations. This book includes the words to the song, and stories and activities about the neighborhood.

In the story "Early Bird on Sesame Street," Big Bird wakes up early in the morning and discovers that a lot happens while Sesame Street sleeps: the bakers bake bread; the fire fighters wash their fire engines; the newspaper seller receives her papers.

"Ernie's Neighborhood" is a story about the fascinating distractions that Ernie encounters in his neighborhood on the way to mail Bert's letter at the post office.

Activities in this book invite children inside some favorite neighborhood places such as "The Shoe Store," "The Pet Store," and "Grover's Restaurant."

Explore your neighborhood with your children so that they can meet your own grocer, baker and mail carrier. Point out the tools of each trade, and your child will be on the way to understanding the neighborhood and how it works.

The Editors
SESAME STREET BOOKS

Early Bird on Sesame Street
It was early morning on Sesame Street.
NO PARKING
123
The sky was still dark.

Everyone was still asleep.
Everyone, that is, except Big Bird.
Big Bird was wide awake.
He sat up in his nest and listened.

He got up and looked around. There was no one to play with.

"Where is everybody?" Big Bird asked. He began to walk. "I'll walk until I find someone to play with," he said.

Big Bird walked up the street and around the corner. When he came to a bakery he stopped. Inside the bakers were taking bread out of the oven. "Everyone there is too busy to play," said Big Bird. So he went on walking.

Big Bird stopped at a firehouse.
The fire fighters were washing the fire engine.
"Everyone here is busy, too," sighed Big Bird. So he went on walking.

Big Bird came to a police station and stopped.

The police officers were standing in a straight line for inspection. "Oh, dear. Everyone is busy this morning," said Big Bird. And he went on walking.

At the newspaper stand the seller was untying bundles of newspapers. "She looks too busy to play," said Big Bird. So he went on walking.

Soon Big Bird came to a window with clocks in it. All the clocks said seven o'clock. "Seven o'clock?" said Big Bird with surprise. "That's the time I usually get up in the morning. I must be an early bird today."

Big Bird walked back to Sesame Street. By the time he got home he was very tired. "I think I will take a little nap," said Big Bird.

"Wake up, Sleepyhead!" said Little Bird. "It's time to get up!"

But Big Bird was fast asleep.

My Street

An address isn't something to wear.
It's the numbers and name that tell you where
To find the place you want to go.
An address tells you what you need to know.

Betty Lou wants to go from her house to 123 Sesame Street to visit Ernie and Bert. Can you help her find her way there? Start at the arrow.

People in Your Neighborhood

These are the people in your neighborhood . . . the people that you meet each day.

invention
Inventor
taxi
OSCAR'S
TAXI
Taxi Driver
petal
stem
leaf
eraser
Science Teacher
Actress
letter
mailbag
Mail Carrier
gas pumps
lift
wrench
Mechanic
comb
scissors
chair
Barber
books
Librarian
trash can
Trash Collector
piano
Music Teacher

People in Your Neighborhood

A TEACHER works the whole day through
To teach important things to you.
He'll teach you things you won't forget
Like numbers and the alphabet.
CDEFGHIJKLM
PQRSTUVWXYZ
PLANETS
A BARBER has a great big chair.
You sit in it, he cuts your hair.
He'll snip and clip and never rest
Until your haircut looks its best.

The BUS DRIVER drives fast or slow
To take you where you want to go.
When you get in and pay your fare
She will drive you anywhere.
YOUR TOOTH
A DENTIST cares for all your teeth,
The top ones and the ones beneath.
So if you have an aching tooth,
He'll fix it quick, and that's the truth.

FIRE FIGHTERS are brave, it's said.
Their engine is a shiny red.
If there's a fire anywhere about
They'll be sure to put it out.
CITY FIRE
Co. No 1
The DOCTOR makes you well real quick
If by chance you're feeling sick.
She works and works the whole day long
To help you feel well and strong.

The GROCER sells the things you eat
Like bread and eggs, cheese and meat.
No matter what you're looking for,
You'll find it at the grocery store.
The SHOEMAKER is always there
To take care of the shoes you wear.
With his hammer, nails, and glue
He'll fix your shoes as good as new.
The CLEANER is the one who knows
How to clean and press your clothes.
He'll take a jacket, suit, or vest
And clean it so you'll look your best.
The TRASH COLLECTOR works each day.
He'll always take your trash away.
He drives the biggest truck you've seen
To keep the city streets all clean.

Find the Hats

Cookie Monster Goes to the Supermarket

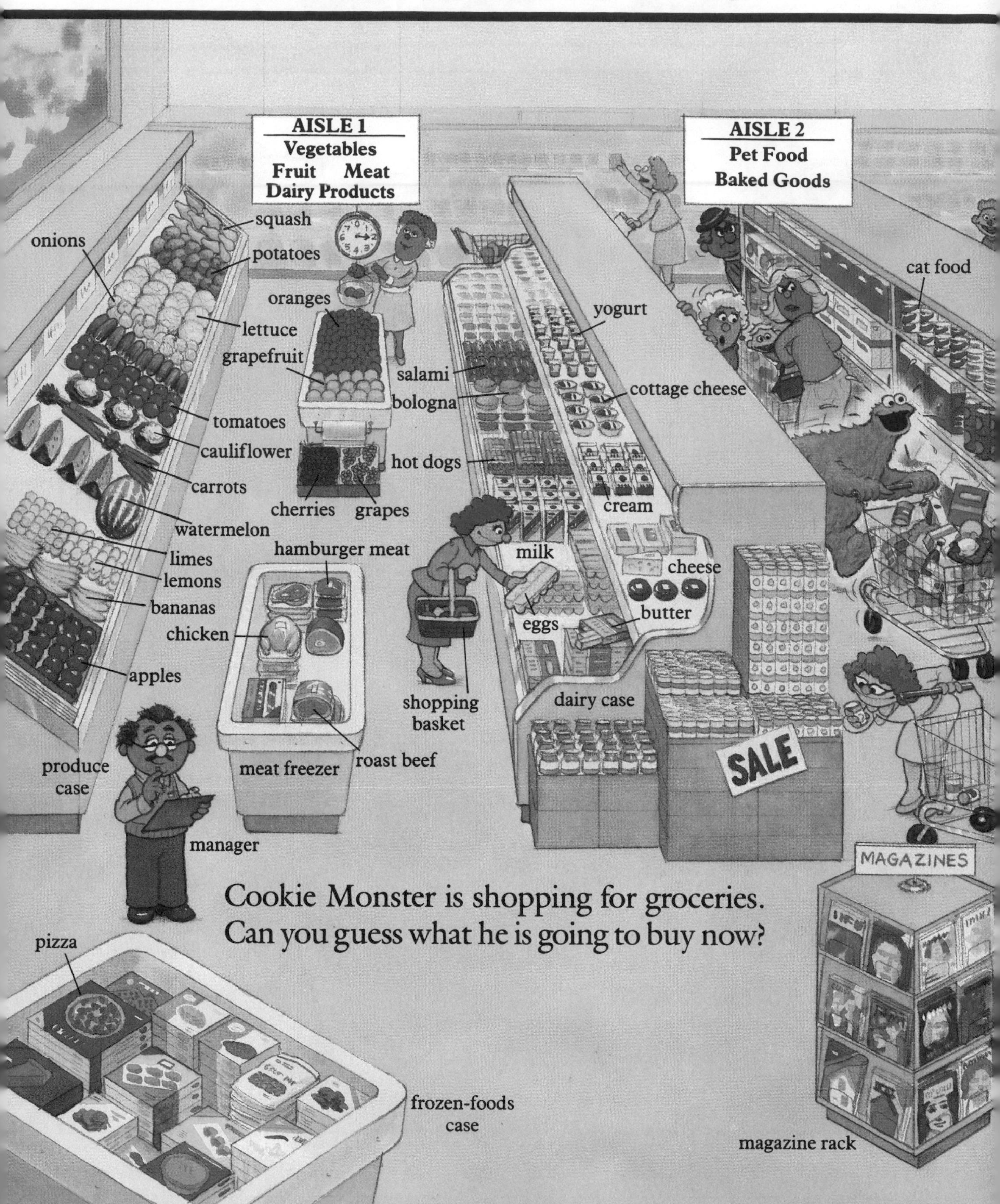

Cookie Monster is shopping for groceries. Can you guess what he is going to buy now?

AISLE 3
Macaroni Cereal
Baking Goods
AISLE 4
Canned Goods
Dry Foods
AISLE 5
Soaps
Detergents
Paper Products
cereal
spaghetti
soup
salt
oatmeal
COOKIES
macaroni
baking powder
baking soda
TUNA ON SALE
cakes
flour
tuna
bread
sugar
doughnuts
cash register
muffins
BOOKS
shopper
ketchup
cashier
jelly
bag
olives
peanut butter
book rack
check-out counter
shopping cart
paper bags

Window Shopping

Look in the windows,
What do you see?
If you could buy a present,
What would it be?

Point to something you would buy your mother.
Point to something you would buy your father.
Point to something you would buy your friend.

The Shoe Store

The Pet Store

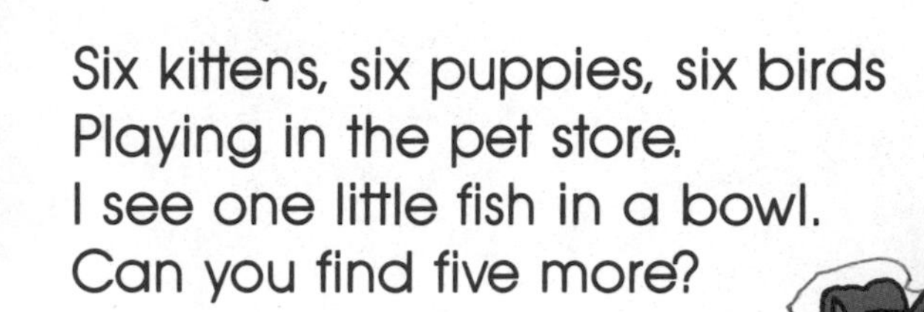

Six kittens, six puppies, six birds
Playing in the pet store.
I see one little fish in a bowl.
Can you find five more?

Which pet would you like
to take home with you?

Sesame Street Block Party

Everyone helps at the
Sesame Street Block Party.
And everyone has lots of fun.

Street Lights

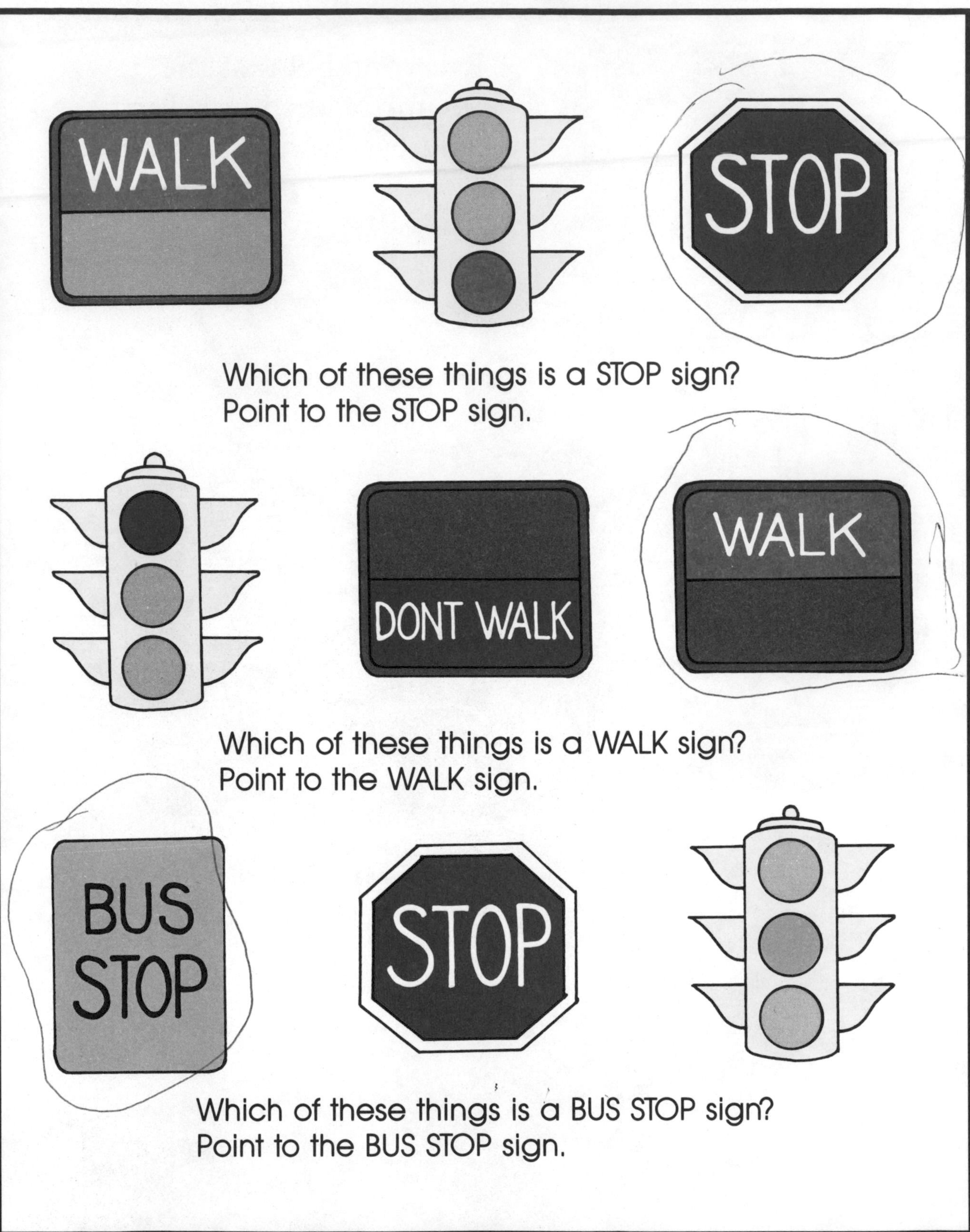

Which of these things is a STOP sign?
Point to the STOP sign.

Which of these things is a WALK sign?
Point to the WALK sign.

Which of these things is a BUS STOP sign?
Point to the BUS STOP sign.

Walk, Don't Walk

Red light, green light; don't walk, walk,
The signs tell us what to do.
But **never** cross the street
Unless a grown-up's helping you!

Betty Lou's mommy takes her across the street
when the sign says WALK.

When can Betty Lou and her mommy cross the street?

Grover's Restaurant

This is a restaurant.
Please take a seat.
The cook will make you
Something to eat.

This is a menu.
I am Grover your waiter.
If you order something now,
I will bring it to you later.

Point to the things you would not find
on a table in a restaurant.

TELE-GRAHAMS

What you need:
whole graham crackers
1 package of cream cheese
½ cup of apple butter

Note: Adult supervision is suggested.

What you do:
Leave the cream cheese out of the refrigerator until it is soft. Then spread each cracker with enough cream cheese to cover it smoothly. Put the apple butter in a plastic sandwich bag, and push it into one corner. Cut a small hole in that corner with your scissors. Gather the bag together around the apple butter, and squeeze the apple butter through the hole to write your message.

CTW
SESAME STR
12345678910

Ernie's Neighborhood

It was a busy Saturday morning on Sesame Street.

David was washing the windows at Hooper's Store.

Susan and Gordon were planting in the little garden in front of 123 Sesame Street.

Big Bird was riding his unicycle.

Ernie was the only one in the neighborhood who wasn't busy.

"Ernie!" Bert called from the window. "Would you please mail this letter at the post office?"

"Sure, Bert," said Ernie.

"It's my entry in the Bottlecap Collectors' Contest," said Bert. "The first prize is a trip to the Figgy Fizz Bottling Company. The envelope has to be mailed today, and I promised I'd help Susan and Gordon plant their garden. Can you get there by twelve o'clock? That's when the post office closes."

"You can count on me, old buddy!" said Ernie.

As Ernie passed Oscar's can Bruno was tossing trash into a big blue sanitation truck.

"Trash pick-up day is my favorite day of the week!" said Oscar. "Look at all this great junk I saved."

"That's nice, Oscar," said Ernie. "But I can't stay. I have to go to the post office to mail this important letter for Bert."

Ernie walked on. As he hurried past the library he heard the librarian reading a story.

"Rumpelstiltskin is my name," she read.

"It's Story Hour!" he said to himself. "Mrs. Anderson is reading my favorite story."

Ernie sat down on the library steps and listened to the story until the end.

Ernie waved at the manager of Playful Pets as he passed by.

"I don't have time to stop today," he called.

Ernie stopped in the pet store for just a little while.

As Ernie waited at a red light a fire truck zoomed by.

"I wonder where the fire truck is going?" he thought.

Then he followed it.

The fire truck drove to the fire station and parked inside. Ernie saw the fire fighters climb off the truck. He watched them wash and polish the fire truck.

"Want to help?" asked the captain. He handed Ernie a soft cloth. "You can give that brass bell a good shine!"

In the playground outside the Sesame Street School, kids were playing games. Grover and some friends were playing softball.

Ernie stopped to watch Herry Monster at bat. Herry swung and hit the ball. It flew high over the fence.

"I've got it!" cried Ernie, and he ran to catch the ball. After the game, Ernie passed Mr. McIntosh's fruit and vegetable stand. Mr. McIntosh was taking shiny red apples out of a crate and stacking them.

"Hi, Ernie," said Mr. McIntosh. "Do you want an apple today?"

"Thanks, Mr. McIntosh," said Ernie. "I'll eat it on my way to the post office. I have to mail an important letter for my buddy Bert."

On his way again, Ernie munched his apple. Then he heard a loud whistle from behind the fence at a construction site. "I'll just peek in," he said.

"The construction site is the busiest place in the neighborhood!" said Ernie. He watched a huge crane lift buckets of cement to the top of the building. "I'd sure like to run a big crane like that someday," said Ernie.

As Ernie hurried past Hooper's Store he spotted a sign in the window.

"Monsterberry Crunch is the flavor of the week. My favorite," he said. "Maybe I'll have just one scoop."

Cuckoo! Cuckoo!

"Where's that bird?" Ernie wondered. He followed the sound to the Fix-It Shop.

"Luis! What is that noise?" asked Ernie.

"It's Bob's cuckoo clock," said Luis. "I'm fixing it. Listen."

A bird popped in and out of the clock. "When it sings cuckoo twelve times, that means it's twelve o'clock."

"TWELVE O'CLOCK!" cried Ernie. "Oh, no! I have to get Bert's letter to the post office."

Ernie ran out of the Fix-It Shop and down the street.

Ernie's feet pounded up the steps of the post office. He imagined he could hear the cuckoo clock chiming twelve already.

It seemed to Ernie that he could never get there before the post office closed.

He raced up to a counter. "Please, I have to mail Bert's Figgy Fizz letter," he said to the postal worker. "I promised to mail it today. I ran and ran to get here by twelve." Ernie stopped, out of breath.

"Don't worry," she said. "Your letter will go out today. You made it just in time."

"Oh, thank you!" said Ernie.

SESAME

When Ernie got back to Sesame Street, Bert said, "You missed a busy morning on Sesame Street. Did you mail my letter in time, Ernie?"

"Sure, Bert," said Ernie. "No problem!"

CTW
SESAME STREET®